WITWOO

AUTHOR: BRIGHT MASIH
ILLUSTRATOR: HANNAH WHITEHEAD

www.fireflystardustbooks.co.uk

ISBN 978-1-7391163-2-3

FIREFLY
STARDUST BOOKS

This book belongs to Miss/Master

....

Dedicated To My Nephew & Nieces.

Hugo

Amelie

&

Esther

x

subscribe at **fireflystardustbooks.co.uk** to be sent the free audiobook.

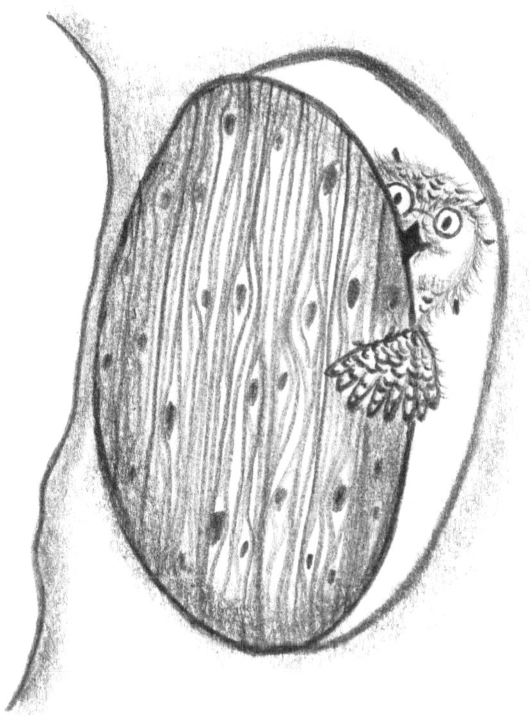

Chapter 1

WitWoo Remembers Something Important!

Silvery moonbeams sliced through the darkness in the heart of the forest. It was dark, not just any kind of dark, but the kind of darkness that makes your tummy feel gurgly and your bottom lip feel trembly. Some creatures don't mind the dark, and WitWoo, the snowy owl was one of them. WitWoo wasn't frightened! No, WitWoo loved the dark and loved to fly through each and every moonbeam!

WitWoo's feathers shimmered in the inky blackness. As he flew through the moonlight, his call echoed through ancient trees, across silent lakes and over snowcapped mountains. WitWoo noticed it had started to snow. Thick, fluffy, pom-pommy snowflakes, the kind that he loved. The snow just continued to fall, softly and silently, draping everything beneath.

Within a few hours, everything that was hard was white and soft. WitWoo stretched out his giant wings, lifted his talons and came to a silent, arcing, gentle stop. Perching high on a tree branch, he sighed and stared at the beauty unfolding beneath him. He just loved it here, deep in the heart of his forest. After a few moments' rest, he took off for home, silently rising higher, higher and higher with each stroke of his wings until all that was above him was the moon and her twinkling, tiny stars.

Waking late the next morning, WitWoo realised he felt cold. Outside, snow had turned to ice, and his little treehouse shivered in the hard morning sunlight. WitWoo's hand-knitted duvet was filled with his old feathers, but even so, he felt chilly. He shivered from head to toe, then pulled it up to his fluffy neck to stay toasty warm. *That's it!* thought WitWoo. *Time to light the fire. I'm freezing!* Floating softly downstairs in an ever-decreasing circle, as if attached to an invisible string, WitWoo softly landed inside his stony living-room fireplace.

WitWoo arranged dried twigs and leaves as kindling, then carefully heaped on knobbly ash logs, which had dried all summer long. Lighting the makeshift kindling, WitWoo watched as tiny yellow sparks flickered into life, then puffed silently into flame. WitWoo listened as the twigs caught and crackled. He loved the sound of crackling fires, and their earthy smell, too.

Before long, WitWoo's cosy little study was glowing shades of orange, amber and red; it was toastie warm. Relaxing into his wingback armchair, he decided it was time for his favourite breakfast: sticky-sweet orange marmalade on thickly buttered brown toast, all washed down with piping hot sugary tea!

Licking his beak and smiling to himself, tasting the last lick of sweetness from his delicious breakfast, WitWoo felt happy, warm and content. Stretching out his thick feathery legs, he wondered what he should do with the rest of his day, just as his eyelids started to feel heavy and then...softly...closed.

By the time WitWoo awoke, shaking the sleep from his large feathery head, it was already midday, and the warming sun was already high up in its wintery sky. *This will never do!* thought WitWoo, stretching his wings and turning his head right round, in the peculiar way only owls do! *I have to make the best of the day! I wonder if there is time for a bath before venturing out?* he pondered.

WitWoo hopped up his creaky oak stairs, into his wooden bathroom then ran the hot and cold porcelain taps, pouring chocolate scented bubble bath into his huge copper tub. The windows steamed up as WitWoo wrote his name on the glass inside a heart, then smiled. Hopping in with a loud wet plop, sliding deep into the warm bath until only his talons and eyes were peeping over the bubbles. The frothy water stuck WitWoo's eyelashes together as he relaxed. Then a thought suddenly popped into his big wet head as he abruptly stood up! *My word, if I'm not mistaken, today is my 50th birthday! I wonder if anyone even remembers?* WitWoo dwelt on this thought and started to feel sad as he slowly lay back down in the bubbles.

The snow sparkled brightly in the midday sun as Mummy Bear and Snowball trudged steadily through it. Walking behind Mummy Bear, Snowball stared at how big Mummy Bear's footprints were compared to his. *They look so huge*, thought Snowball, as he decided it could be fun to walk in them, just as Mummy Bear made them. Snowball proceeded to do this, with some measure of success, if only for a while. 'I can't believe I will ever have feet that big, even when I'm growned up!' said Snowball out loud.

'What are you doing back there, Snowball?' asked Mummy Bear, stopping suddenly, turning to face her mischievous cub. 'Nothing,' whispered Snowball under his breath as he walked straight into Mummy Bear's tummy, falling backwards in a furry white heap at her feet, looking up. Mummy Bear decided it was time for Snowball's rest, so they sat on an old oak bench as Mummy Bear gently stroked Snowball's soft white head, which he always loved.

'What you and Squeak are doing for WitWoo is really kind, Snowball. I'm proud of you,' said Mummy Bear. WitWoo was the nearest thing to a daddy for Snowball, as he was always there for Mummy Bear and Snowball, especially when they needed him the most. Deep down, Snowball felt that he loved WitWoo, and his tummy told him that WitWoo loved him too.

After a while, they decided it was probably time to eat their packed lunches, which were packed carefully in Mummy Bear's knapsack: deliciously crunchy peanut butter sandwiches, sugary iced buns with sticky strawberry jam and warm hot chocolate topped with cream and marshmallows, Snowball's particular favourite. 'Right, time to carry on, Snowball! said Mummy Bear, wiping the chocolate off his furry white face. 'We have a lot to do before tonight, we can't leave it all to Squeak and the others.' They stood up, and off they trudged, crunching through the deep white snow, now with full, happy tummies.

CHAPTER 2

SQUEAKS BIG PARTY PREPARATIONS

Squeak felt sad and was starting to feel a little sorry for himself, if he was completely honest. Feeling exhausted, there he lay, sprawled on a pile of colourful felt bunting, staring wistfully at the pointy roof of the recently erected wigwam. As he daydreamed, colourful wooden lanterns, tied high in the tree trunks, swayed gently in the breeze, as Squeak rubbed his velvety black forehead.

How are we ever going to finish all of this? he thought. *There is just so much left to do!* Squeak had been up since sunrise, squeaking this way and that way, as he busily worked, leaving glittery sparkling trails everywhere, as you know baby penguins always do. *'Snowball's going to be here soon, and there is so much left for me to do!'* Squeak was Snowball's best friend, and he wanted ever so much to please him; after all, he had promised that he would do his best to help.

Squeak felt this was the least he could do, especially after Mummy Bear and Snowball had discovered him, covered beak to feet in sweet sugary icing, cake crumbs and sticky blueberry jam. Yes, Squeak was caught red handed, eating cakes that Mummy Bear had baked only the previous day! The mystery of where the cakes had gone was solved by opening the door to his wardrobe, where Squeak secretly sat, feasting.

Even earlier the previous day, Daddy Penguin had found some old birch tree trunks that had toppled down in the last of the heavy snowstorms. With the help of Mummy Bear, Daddy Penguin had positioned them all so that they made a huge, spoked circle of trunks, which looked like an enormous bicycle wheel made for giants!

Squeak looked at Daddy Penguin, and then the circle, and then back at Daddy Penguin and thought, *What is Daddy doing, this really isn't helping me?* shrugging his little black velvety shoulders and rolling his grey eyes. Then, Daddy Penguin brought together all the trunk ends in the centre of the circle and tied them together with a strong, thick, heavy rope.

'Everyone, grab a trunk then walk forward slowly together, please, sliding your trunk as you go!' They all did as Daddy Penguin asked, sliding the other ends of the trunks on the snow-covered floor, as the tree trunks started to magically stand up at an angle!

Squeak was astounded with his mouth wide open and his fins on his hips! Standing inside the trunks, which towered over him, Daddy Penguin cleared his throat, raised his fins and proudly announced to them all, 'May I present to you, one and all, an A grade, Daddy Penguin speciality wigwam!' Then he bowed his shiny black head, almost touching his feet, as his bowler hat tumbled off! Squeak remembered how everyone had clapped and smiled in amazement as the magical tree trunk structure rose up out of the ground and formed a wigwam. Squeak, Mummy Penguin and the others then set to work, covering it with an assortment of twigs, leaves, branches and berries, finally hanging big wooden lanterns from the top of the trunks, on long swaying ropes.

Squeak and the others had certainly worked hard, but Squeak himself had cut out and sewn together all the colourful bunting and carefully tied all the lanterns to the tops of the tree trunks, ready to be lit later. Squeak had even covered the ground in freshly dried fern leaves so that the wigwam smelt lovely, and he had put up all the birthday banners that they had painted together with cherry juice only the previous evening.

Meanwhile, Mummy Bear and Mummy Penguin had worked hard too and baked lots of lovely cakes. This time, they made sure little Squeak was nowhere near them, just in case he found himself in trouble, due to that famously sweet tooth of his, which often led him astray.

There were delicious Battenberg cakes, tempting angel cakes, gooey chocolate cakes, but best of all, in the middle of them all, a giant iced birthday cake, shaped into the form of a huge snowy owl covered in white edible glitter. Its outstretched leaves were adorned in all manner of nuts, with yellow marzipan eyes and black pupils made of sweet liquorice!

Squeak spent the rest of the afternoon dreaming of how that cake would have tasted, and as he worked, busily preparing the wigwam, he often looked over his little black shoulder wistfully at the iced owl cake as he felt his heart beat faster and faster. 'That's not for you just yet, Squeak my boy!' said Daddy Penguin. 'It's for our guest of honour, so be a good chap and leave it be!' He patted his head gently as he shuffled busily by. Squeak loved Daddy Penguin, he always made him feel safe.

Chapter 3

WitWoo Flies, Downwards!

Having enjoyed his bubble bath, WitWoo spent a long time drying himself with his favourite scratchy towel. It's just not that easy for an owl to get perfectly dry. First, he dried his feathery round head, then his pointy little ears, face and beak, then under his big wide belly, then finally, his feathery legs and tail feathers, too.

WitWoo stared through the steamed-up window and watched as the sun set lower and lower in the darkening amber sky. He felt as though he could feel the warmth being turned down as the sun met the land and the stars peaked through the glowing fabric of the evening sky.

WitWoo stared in sudden shock as he noticed the reflection of his grandfather clock, ticking over to seven in the evening! 'My word,' exclaimed WitWoo, 'have I really been in the bath that long? I thought I had only been bathing for a short while!' In reality, WitWoo had spent nearly four long, lazy hours in his bubbly tub, frequently topping it up with hot frothy water, and his favourite chocolate bubble bath mixture.

I Love Chocolate
CHOCOL
Bubble
SOAP

Now dry, WitWoo swiftly flew downstairs and slowly creaked open the door to his tree house, staring up at a sea of twinkling stars, stretching across the wide expansive sky. Even after all the years that had passed, in what had seemed a blink of an eye, WitWoo still loved staring into the pin cushioned sky, and he often wondered what stars actually were, whether they where hot or cold.

That evening, fern scented trees, deep in the magical forest, laced the cool night air with a refreshing fragrance. WitWoo spread his wings out wide and stamped his right foot seven times, blinking his right eye at the same time! With a puff of green, starry, glittery smoke, he magically disappeared, leaving his treehouse suddenly empty!

With a second glittery puff, WitWoo suddenly reappeared, soaring high above the treetops, held invisibly within the night sky. WitWoo is a magical owl, you see, in the way that the best owls always are. WitWoo corkscrewed happily through the air as it ruffled and tickled the feathers on his broad white face. He chuckled to himself as he flew, tumbling, turning and looping!

WitWoo just loved to fly, especially at nighttime, when all the stars and the moon reflected the joy in his huge, happy, owly eyes. As he was flying, WitWoo noticed something new in his forest. He swooped down steeply to take a closer look. Spreading his wings wide and pushing himself back against the wind, slowing his fall and stretching out his talons, a moment later he gently landed, soft as a feather, on a branch of a tall pine tree covered in fresh heavy snow.

Peering down between his talons WitWoo saw the strangest thing, what looked like a huge wooden cone made of tree trunks covered in leaves, branches and berries. Through it, WitWoo thought he saw pin pricks of glowing amber light, swaying in the breeze, which attracted nearby moths and fireflies, curiously fluttering all over it!

WitWoo closed his eyes. Gripping firmly onto the branch, then he softly let himself fall backwards. He was now upside down, gently swinging like a giant feathery bat. There was no mistaking it, breathing in deeply he smelt his favourite smell in the whole wide world: CHOCOLATE!

WitWoo thought he must have been imagining it, so he let himself dream just a little while longer. He dreamt he was flying over a sea of warm flowing chocolate custard, with wide round islands made of his favourite treat, Christmas pudding. As WitWoo dreamt, he fell fast asleep, and then without even realising it, he relaxed his talons and accidentally let go of the branch he was clinging to, snoring gently as he suddenly fell!

Chapter 4

Happy Birthday, WitWoo!

Squeak looked up in amazement; they had finally finished. The wigwam was now awash with colourful bunting, glowing lit lanterns and tinsel made of intertwined leaves, mixed with colourful wintery flowers and bright red holly berries. Mummy Bear had laid a huge round table full of cakes, and of course, mugs of hot chocolate.

In pride of place, in the centre of the table, was the giant owl cake, which Squeak just couldn't wait to eat. In fact, he had been daydreaming about it most of the afternoon after discovering it earlier!

'Right,' said Mummy Bear, 'we better go and call on WitWoo. We're late, he will never have expected any of this for his birthday!'

'Come on, children,' replied Mummy Penguin, 'it's time to go and surprise him!' Suddenly, just as Mummy Penguin had finished speaking and reached out for Squeak's little fin, there was an almighty crash! Out of nowhere, with a loud squelchy plop, WitWoo plummeted headfirst deep into his life-sized cake, with his feathery legs and talons poking curiously out of the top! Then, suddenly, WitWoo awoke!

WitWoo felt dazed and confused! One minute he was having a delicious sleepy dream, dangling upside down. The next minute he was waking up, knee deep inside what felt and tasted bizarrely like chocolate cake. WitWoo licked his beak, tasting rich, creamy chocolate, then he felt a strong hard tug on his feathery legs. Suddenly, with a loud wet squelch, he was pulled free from the owl cake, and he found himself standing beside it.

WitWoo slowly opened his eyes and stared around the wigwam and wondered if he was still dreaming. All thoughts of being embarrassed dissolved as he saw the warm smiling faces of those he loved the most. Staring back at him was Mummy Bear with little Snowball. Mummy and Daddy Penguin, with little Squeak and little Ambrose with Mummy and Daddy Fox.

'Was this all for me?' asked WitWoo, pointing with his wings. 'Happy birthday, WitWoo!' said Squeak as he pulled the twine that released a net up above holding thousands of oak leaves, which twisted, turned and flew all around them. WitWoo lay on his back next to his birthday cake and watched the oak leaves flying all around him, totally oblivious of everyone staring at him!

As the last of the leaves gently fell to the floor of the wigwam, WitWoo rubbed his teary eyes, stood up and cleared his throat. He thought deep and hard about what he should say. Walking up to his friends, WitWoo hugged each one of them in turn, then spoke.

When I woke up this morning, I felt old and sad, but thanks to you, my sweet dear friends, I feel loved and happy. Thank you so much, I love you all.' WitWoo kissed Snowball, Squeak and Ambrose on their little heads and smiled broadly at their parents. 'Well, I think there's only one thing left to say,' said Mummy Bear as she suddenly appeared with a round birthday cake lit with 50 flickering candles.

'HAPPY BIRTHDAY TO YOU... HAPPY BIRTHDAY TO YOU... HAPPY BIRTHDAY, DEAR WITWOO... HAPPY BIRTHDAY... TO...YOU.'

With that, everybody cheered and shouted, 'Hip, hip hooray! Hip, hip hooray! Hip, hip hooray!' WitWoo gently closed his eyes, blew out the candles and smiled, feeling safe, warm and loved, smelling CHOCOLATE, his most favourite smell of all!

The End.

Other books in The Firefly Adventures Series

Book 1

Has Anybody Seen Snowball?

Book 2

WitWoo

Book 3

Sweet Tooth Squeak

About the Author

Growing up in the '70s, during the height of racial tensions, wasn't always easy, but my mother and father, Anwar and Khursheidan, made the most out of what they had. Through their iron clad Christian faith, they always tried to do the best for my siblings and me.

As a child my days were spent joyfully playing marbles with other children on metal manhole covers, British Bulldog in the middle of the road and going on long bike rides through the tall, deep woods, during what felt like the endlessly sunny summer school holidays.

What I wish to do through my books, even if only for a few moments, is to transport children to a place where they can daydream with feelings of curiosity, amazement and joy, in the same way my friends and I did when I was a boy. When the world, at least to me and my little friends, felt like a happier, simpler place, where our imaginations were not supplemented by smartphones or the Internet, but simply by curiosity.

Ingram Content Group UK Ltd.
Milton Keynes UK
UKHW051017290623
424230UK00004B/27